Mel Bay Presents

Shady Grove

Acoustic Guitar Solos by **Jerry GARCIA**

with Melodies, Lyrics, and Chords

transcribed by Dix Bruce

A compact disc (98718CD) of the music in this book is now available. The publisher strongly recommends the use of these recordings along with the text to insure accuracy of interpretation and ease in learning.

The CD is produced by Acoustic Disc Records.

2 3 4 5 6 7 8 9 0

Visit us on the Web at www.melbay.com — E-mail us at email@melbay.com

Contents

Introduction

To say that the Grateful Dead are a cultural phenomenon is like saying that the Beatles were a little band from England. The importance of the Dead in popular culture has been immense for decades and continues, nearly as strong as ever, years after their final performance.

Jerry Garcia, the lead guitarist, singer, and alleged leader of the band, became an icon of the 60s youth movement, and as he aged, attained an elder statesman status, a living reminder and symbol of all the things that various fans wanted to attribute to that era: the good the bad and the ugly. That he rejected responsibility or leadership of any kind is well-known. He just wanted to play music.

It was also well known that Jerry was a huge fan, and probably considered himself a player, of old-time American music, from mountain fiddle and banjo music, to sea chanteys, to English ballads, to jug band music to bluegrass and blues, encompassing everything in between and on either side. He absorbed all that he heard and honed his music craft in many folk and traditional bands before the Dead.

I have heard him quoted as saying that the Dead were just playing this same folk music in a slightly different form, with their own arrangements and additions. They didn't necessarily set out to play pop music or rock and roll; they wanted simply to play music that they loved and much of that was based on traditional folk music.

Of course, at the time, playing folk music on electric instruments at high volume was unacceptable and sacrilegious to the folk scene. Bob Dylan was branded a "traitor" when he "went electric." That prejudice survives to this day. But electric instruments were the coin of the popular music realm. They were readily available and completely accepted in the youth and rock scenes that would be the main audience for groups like the Dead. And, it was much easier to make yourself heard with a plugged-in electric Gibson than with an unplugged acoustic Martin. I'm sure electric instruments also offered interesting tonal possibilities to the Dead as well as the chance to meld the traditional music they loved with current styles and conventions. Their use of electricity and volume was so antithetical to the folk-powers-that-be that they slipped into an entirely different genre. Whether it was called folk/rock, San Francisco Rock, or Psychedelia, the perception of the music changed and it was clearly no longer folk or old-time.

The predominant thought that struck me as I studied Garcia's playing on "Shady Grove" was how close his and David Grisman's versions of the songs were to those of the original musicians they learned from. The popular media view of the 1960s era and groups like the Dead was "anything goes and we'll make it up as we go along." One might agree with that assessment, especially after hearing the Dead render a ten, fifteen minute, or longer ride on one song. And, there was very little about their music that sounded like Roscoe Holcomb or Mississippi John Hurt.

But on the "Shady Grove" recordings one can hear the deep commitment, respect, and love Jerry had for this traditional American music. He's very faithful to the original artists' music. That surprised me a bit, I guess because I expected more of an ego-driven "my version" approach from one the biggest rock stars ever. What you have here is a vibrant collection of wonderful traditional American songs, from a great variety of genres, played in a style closely based on their traditional sources. Of course within those parameters we hear wonderful and personal readings of the tunes from both Jerry and David.

David and I go back quite a few years. I was a big fan of his ground breaking David Grisman Quintet (DGQ) in the mid-1970s. Living in the San Francisco Bay Area provided me with ample opportunity to see the group develop from its earliest. I'd listened to David on record with Red Allen, The Muleskinner Band, and The Even Dozen Jug Band, among others, and first heard him perform live in the band that immediately preceded his DGQ, The Great American Music Band. Eventually I met David and the other band members and began working for **Mandolin World News**, David's legendary magazine. I edited it from 1978 to 1984. (It ceased publication in 1985. Back issues are available from Musix, PO Box 231005, Pleasant Hill, CA 94523 or e-mail: info@musixnow.com) He was a strong and generous influence on my music and my life. And, it goes without saying, he is a great mandolin player and composer. It's a treat to hear him with Jerry.

I transcribed Jerry's playing after carefully listening to each selection many times. I tried to determine not just *what* he was playing but *how* he was playing it. Certain sounds on a guitar can only be played at one place on the fretboard and I did my best to note all these instances in the tablature.

Of course, there are many places in the music

where it's impossible to tell exactly in which position Jerry played a certain passage. In deciding where to place the tablature numbers, I analyzed the sounds on the CD and tried to balance what I heard with likely fretboard positions and playability. I assumed that Jerry played the acoustic cutaway guitar shown on page three of the CD booklet on at least some of the tracks. That type of guitar would have given him easy access to the uppermost frets on the fingerboard. However, David tells me that Jerry played a variety of guitars, with and without cutaways, on the sessions.

The CD booklet, with notes by New Lost City Rambler John Cohen, is packed with excellent information on both Jerry and David and their backgrounds in traditional American music. It offers an engaging perspective on how they got from their formative folkie years to the music you are now enjoying and also addresses how the music for which they are famous—Jerry with the Grateful Dead and David with his dawg music—relate to these early influences. Cohen also offers great history on and insight into the songs themselves which adds an important dimension to the transcriptions that follow. My first suggestion is that you listen to the music and read the notes! My comments will generally be confined on how to play these pieces on guitar.

My job was to transcribe the melodies, lyrics, chords, and many of the solos on these recordings and prepare versions playable on the guitar. I tried to represent melodies as closely as possible and still have them be readable. On the songs where Jerry played banjo and not guitar, I adapted his banjo part to be playable on the guitar. Of course one can't totally capture on the page all that's being played and sung on the CD. We just don't have the notation technology and it's impossible to communicate all the subtleties of old-time music fully with spots and stems. You gotta listen and after you listen you gotta play it and sing it!

The small numbers between the notation and tablature staves indicate suggested fretting-hand fingers to use to play the notes. I tried to keep these to a minimum to avoid jumbling up the music too much. Most fingerings should be obvious and you should feel free to develop your own. "h" = hammer on, "p" = pull off, "s" = slide, "b" = string bend. If there are several identical notations in a row in the music, I only included the first one or two. Measure numbers are indicated in the music once per staff above the left hand measure. Measure numbers are referred to in the text in this way: "M 4" = "measure four."

Extra special thanks are due to Laura Alber, Robert Bergman, and Charlotte Gibb for their most helpful suggestions and assistance in preparing this book. They have the eyes of eagles!

So, read along and play along and have a great time with Jerry Garcia and David Grisman. You can write to me c/o MUSIX, PO Box 231005, Pleasant Hill, CA 94523 or e-mail: Dix@musixnow.com

Dix Bruce
June 2002

Dix Bruce

Dix Bruce is a musician and writer from the San Francisco Bay Area. He has authored over thirty books, recordings, and videos for Mel Bay Publications. He edited David Grisman's "Mandolin World News" from 1978 to 1984. He does studio work on guitar, mandolin, and banjo and has recorded two LPs with mandolin legend Frank Wakefield, eight big band CDs with the Royal Society Jazz Orchestra, his own collection of American folk songs entitled "My Folk Heart" on which he plays guitar, mandolin, autoharp and sings, and a CD of string swing & jazz entitled "Tuxedo Blues." He contributed two original compositions to the soundtrack of Harrod Blank's acclaimed documentary "Wild Wheels." He has released two CDs of traditional American songs and originals with guitarist Jim Nunally.

Dix Bruce arranged, composed, played mandolin, and recorded music for the CD ROM computer game "The Sims" for the Maxis Corporation. His music is featured on a virtual radio station within the game.

Dix's latest books for Mel Bay Publications are *Great Mandolin Pickin' Tunes*, (book & CD set MB98420BCD) an eclectic collection of tunes for mandolin including Classical, Bluegrass, Gospel, Cajun, Ethnic, Christmas, Jazz, Irish, Old-Time, Italian, and Ragtime selections; *Guide to Capo, Transposing, & the Nashville Numbering System*, (MB98413) a comprehensive explanation of music theory for guitarists which includes all the subjects mentioned in the title; and *BackUP TRAX: Basic Blues for Guitar* — a book and play along CD set which teaches fourteen blues tunes in a variety of classic styles, including Country and Urban Blues, Acoustic and Electric Blues, Delta Blues, Texas Blues, Chicago Blues, Slide Guitar Blues, Alternate Tuning, Traditional and Modern Blues. Students learn by jamming along with a hot blues band (guitar, bass, drums, keys, harmonica). Melodies are presented in the book with chords, standard notation, and tablature and recorded on the CD at both slow and regular speeds. Then the band plays backup while the student plays all the leads --- melodies or licks and riffs from the book or the student's own solos. His two newest instructional videos are from Stefan Grossman's Guitar Workshop and are titled *Basic Country Flatpicking Guitar* (MB99414VX) and *Basic Swing Guitar* (MB99416VX).

Dix Bruce
(photo by Jon Sievert)

Also by Dix Bruce:

CDs, videos, and instructional books by Dix Bruce: (For songlists and full details, contact Musix, PO Box 231007, Pleasant Hill, CA 94523. E-mail: info@musixnow.com).

String Band Classics: The Fuzzy Mountain String Band for Mandolin, Guitar (MB#96687BCD) book & CD sets of transcriptions: chords, melodies, lyrics, solos.

Doc Watson & Clarence Ashley 1960-62 for Guitar (book & CD set of transcriptions: chords, melodies, lyrics, Doc's solos & rhythm playing, incredible repertoire).

You Can Teach Yourself Country Guitar book, book & CD, tape, or video set (MB#94818).

BackUp Trax: Old Time Fiddle Tunes Vol. I book & CD set. (MB#94339BCD) Jam all night long with the band on old-time and fiddle tunes. You play all the leads and the band never gets tired!

Beginning Country Guitar Handbook–Basic Flatpicking book & CD set.

BackUp Trax: Swing & Jazz Vol. I book & CD set. (MB#94344BCD) Jam all night long with a great band.

BackUp Trax: Traditional Jazz & Dixieland book & CD set. Jam all night long with the band on the basic Dixieland repertoire.

BackUp Trax: Early Jazz & Hot Tunes book & CD set. Jam all night long with the band on more traditional jazz standards.

You Can Teach Yourself Mandolin book, cassette, CD, or video (MB#94331).

Basic Country Flatpicking Guitar video (Stefan Grossman's Guitar Workshop)(MB#99414VX).

Basic Swing Guitar video (Stefan Grossman's Guitar Workshop)(MB#99416VX).

The Songs

1. Shady Grove (page 10) is the title tune of the set and a wonderful old song that's played in all sorts of old-time, folk, and bluegrass contexts with a variety of arrangements: from modal, like this one, to major key, driving bluegrass versions. The Garcia/Grisman version is quite similar Doc Watson's and Clarence Ashley's, which you'll find in my book of transcriptions "Doc Watson & Clarence Ashley: 1960-1962" (Mel Bay Publications)

I transcribed all of Jerry's solos. I think it's interesting to study how he develops the theme of the melody over the various repetitions. He does this very much in the old-time tradition changing his solos only slightly while maintaining a clear concept of the melody.

The parentheses around the B note in M 4 mean that Jerry plays this note very lightly. He plays similar light notes in M 55-56. The second half of the second solo, which begins in M 33, makes liberal use of hammers and pulls, noted with "h" and "p."

In M 3 and 11, you can either slide into the D note on the fifth string fifth fret or play the open fourth string D notes.

The third guitar solo, which begins in M 49, is interesting and challenging. The whole thing is played up the neck in closed position, all fretted notes with no open string notes. Again, having not seen Jerry play these songs, I'm not positive about the tablature positions. Obviously on some of these passages there are up to three position choices.

You'll notice a little "tent" above the second note of M 33 and the fourth note of M 49 which Jerry really blasts out, hence the accent mark above it. The second note in M 52 is probably a goof. Normally one would play an F natural over the Dm chord, not an F♯.

Throughout this entire set of songs, Jerry's chord strums are very light, sometimes almost imperceptible. Keep that in mind as you play through the solos.

2. Stealin' (page 16) comes from the Memphis Jug Band and is one of my all time favorites. (You can hear the original recording that Jerry and David heard in the early 1960s on the RCA CD "Wild About My Lovin' • Beale Street Blues 1928-1930" (2461-2-R).) Jerry's lead guitar is featured throughout the recording. I transcribed the introduction plus two other solos. M 31 & 32 overlap at the transition between the vocal chorus and the guitar solo. I wanted to show Jerry's descending lick behind the vocal. Timing-wise, you should leave out one measure or the other.

3. Off to Sea Once More (page 20) begins with Jerry's chordal accompaniment to David's mandolin lead. It looks a little scary but it's really just Jerry adding notes to his basic Dm chord. The lead guitar parts are all duets with David. There are a few tricky hammer and pull combinations that will take some practice to coordinate (M 60, 63, 69, etc.). In M 62 & 74, make your regular Dm chord and use your fretting finger to fret the fourth string F melody note.

4. The Sweet Sunny South (page 26) is a popular song among old-time and bluegrass musicians. Its lyrics have an unequaled simple and poetic beauty. I included a version of it in my own "You Can Teach Yourself Country Guitar" (MB94818BCD). Jerry plays banjo on this tune so I've had to adapt his banjo playing for the guitar. I tried to keep his basic approach with its many hammers and slides in tact. The chords in parenthesis (M 14-15; M 28-31) are optional. David and Jerry tend to stay on the G chord, but many old-time and bluegrass musicians go from G to D and back.

5. Louis Collins (page 28) is a fingerpicked song in the traditional style where the thumb picks an alternating bass line while the index finger (and sometimes the middle finger) plays the melody and pattern fills. If both a melody note and the bass note fall on the same beat, the thumb and index finger play with a pinch. I've noted the suggested basic pattern in the first few bars: *t* = thumb; *i* = index; *m* = middle.

Since Jerry was missing most of the middle finger of his right hand, he probably played this tune with his index finger, ring finger and thumb. Some traditional players use only the thumb and index finger and Jerry could have used this combination. However, since he was an accomplished Scruggs-style banjo player used to playing three finger rolls on that instrument, it seems more than likely that he used his thumb, index finger, and ring finger.

As you can see from the marked pattern, I use the middle finger quite a bit. Of course you could play all of these notes with the index finger. How ever you do it, you want to be able to play combinations like the one in M 4 smoothly.

If you are new to this style of playing, "Louis Collins" will be a very big challenge. If you want to work up to it, I suggest that you first work on fingerpicking a few simpler songs like "Railroad Bill" or "Freight Train." Coordinating the fingers and thumb, melody and bass, especially with the syncopation in "Louis Collins" can be difficult. You also need to be able to move your fingers in and out of chord forms to catch alternate bass notes, as on the C chord in M 3. Use the thumb of your fretting hand to fret the low, sixth string F note on the F chord in M 8, 11, 20, etc.

"Louis Collins," which was learned from John Hurt, is poignant and beautiful, a great example of the timelessness and soulfullness of traditional music. If you're interested in hearing more of John Hurt's music from the late 1920s, "The Greatest Songters" (Document CD DOCD-5003) includes "Louis Collins" and twelve other of his original recordings. John Hurt was "re-discovered" in the 1960s when he returned to performing and recorded for the Vanguard label. Elizabeth Cotten, famous for her song "Freight Train," also played in this same basic fingerpicking style and M 10-12 and M 22-24 remind me very much of her sound. The late Ms. Cotten recorded for Folkways. Arhoolie Records has a live Elizabeth Cotten concert CD available.

6. Fair Ellender (page 31) begins with Jerry backing up David's introduction. Jerry plays a basic "bass note/strum" accompaniment pattern with very light strums, really just whispers, most of the time. Also, players in this general flatpicking style rarely strum all six strings of a chord. Rather they'll play a bass note, and in the same motion, strum on the remaining strings. For example, if the bass note is on string six, the strum might be on strings five to one, or four to one, but the player wouldn't reverse his hand motion to include string six in the strum. If the bass note was on string four, the strum might only include strings three to one. To play the low F♯ bass note on the D chord in M 9, use your fretting hand thumb. In M 57, the term "arpeggiate" means to slowly drag the pick over all six string of the chord articulating each note.

7. Jackaroo (page 34) One of the things I like best about this collection is that it encompasses such a wide range of traditional folk music from old-time to ballad to blues to songs of the sea. In the days when Jerry and David were learning, the sense of discovery energized students to be hungry for it all and they absorbed an eclectic mix of many styles. These days people seem to me to be much more limited in their interests and I often hear statements like "I only listen to Delta blues" or "I only want to learn bluegrass." These folks are missing a great deal since each style borrows from and informs the other. And, as this collection demonstrates so well, all these genres have absolutely stunning songs that should not be missed.

Jerry's solo begins in M 23 and it's a humdinger, packed with great melodic ideas and finger moves. If you're a beginning or intermediate player, the lead work will be very challenging. Be of good cheer though, you can still play the chords and sing along. Most of the solo is played in different closed positions, up the neck, with a variety of hammers, pulls, slides and combinations of the three. Again, the tablature is based on my best guesses and logic. Jerry may have played them at different places on the fingerboard. One special challenge, particularly if you aren't used to playing this far up the neck, will be to smoothly move from one position to another. In a couple of passages I suggest fretting finger numbers, shown between the standard and tablature staves, to help you position your hand.

The little "b" in M 38 means to bend the string at the indicated fret. This type of string bending is prevalent in blues and rock guitar playing. The lick in M 4-5 is played between the verses.

8. Casey Jones (page 38) is another fingerpicked classic from John Hurt. It starts out with a four measure vamp pattern on the guitar. Then Jerry and David play a duet one time through on the melody. Jerry plays this same basic part behind his vocals as well. Like "Louis Collins," this piece is very difficult.

In "Louis Collins," the picking pattern used the middle finger extensively. In "Casey Jones" your index finger will get some exercise. Again, you can use your index and middle fingers interchangeably as long as you find a way to smoothly play combinations like those in M 5, 7, 9, etc.

In M 5, you'll see a G note in parenthesis. Here Jerry lightly brushed the open third string. You can leave it out completely if you wish. In M 11, and later in M 46 & 64, you'll need to use the "hoe handle A" chord shown below. M 12, 47 & 65 you'll use the thumb of your fretting hand to fret the low F♯ note on the sixth string second fret.

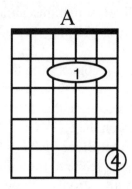

In M 14 Jerry plays a triplet with a hammer on between the first and second notes. This is one tough move and it will take you awhile to integrate it into the flow of the picking. Also in M14, Jerry sometimes plays the D bass note instead of the B at this point in the song.

The solos after verse three begin in M 39. Pretty complicated stuff as Jerry goes up the neck and incorporates various two-string slides on both a bass and melody note. When you see two fretting finger numbers stacked, as in M 40, the lower number refers to the lower note, the upper number to the higher note. In M 44 he mutes the two D bass notes.

The last solo, beginning in M 58, is quite similar to the first solo or what Jerry plays behind his vocal. It's easier to play than the middle solo and it has a few variations from the first, which I think are quite interesting.

9. Dreadful Wind and Rain (page 42) Jerry's playing gets deep on this song. While his solos are very melodic, some of the positions and finger moves are difficult. I've marked several passages with suggested fingerings and positions. The first solo begins in M 13 with the melody. The second solo begins in M 24 and is a restatement of the melody an octave lower and with some slight variations. Jerry plays two D natural notes in M 29, unusual and kind of bluesy against the E major chord. Throughout the solos (M 39, 53, 64) he includes unusual notes that add to the distinctive sound of the solos. The solos beginning in M 37 are loaded with difficult hammers, pulls, and slides.

10. I Truly Understand (page 46) features Jerry on the banjo again, this time in claw hammer style, with David on the guitar. They play an ensemble melody though each interprets it according to the instrument each plays. I've tried to maintain the flavor of the duet in the guitar arrangement. It ends up being an amalgam of both of their parts.

In M 3 and in several other places there's a slide from the fifth string second fret to the third string open. Pick the fretted note and then slide from the second to the fifth fret of the fifth string but sound the D note on the open fourth string. Notice that the entire introduction, just like the verses that follow, is played over a G chord.

11. The Handsome Cabin Boy (page 49) I transcribed all of Jerry's leads, including the intro and ending, so you can study his subtle melodic variations over the course of the song. The trick to playing these solos is to keep your fretting hand in the basic shape of the given chord. Use the closest fretting hand finger to fret the melody notes that aren't part of the held chord. For example, in M 2 you'll use the unused

fourth finger to fret the fourth string fourth fret F# melody note. To play the E note that follows in that same measure, you'll pull your first finger from the chord and use it to fret the fourth string second fret E while holding the remainder of the D chord with fingers two and three. In M 98 and elsewhere you'll find slides from a fretted to an open note, just like in "I Truly Understand."

12. Whisky in the Jar (page 56) gives you a good dose of Jerry's accompaniment guitar playing behind David in both the introduction and on an instrumental chorus (beginning in M 68). Once again you'll need to use your thumb to play the low sixth string F bass note in M 5 and elsewhere. In M 18 he changes from a G to a G7 chord in mid-measure.

The guitar solo, M 51, uses lots of hammers and pulls and integrates them into the fabric of the melody.

13. Down in the Valley (page 60) is recognized all over the country as one of the folkiest of folksongs. It has been taught in schools, sung in homes and around campfires through most of the 20th century. Everyone knows it, sings it, and loves it. It's fitting that Jerry and David end their official set with this song.

The guitar work is quite typical of Jerry in this collection and if you've been playing through the solos up to this point, it should give you no trouble. In M 59, the whole band, led by Jerry's guitar, begins to *ritard* or slow down. In the last three measures Jerry simply strums chords.

14. Hesitation Blues (page 63) If you keep listening past about 5:55 on "Down in the Valley," you'll find an unlisted bonus track, "Hesitation Blues." It's a classic blues, jug band and old-time song that everyone ought to know! I started the transcription after the fade in and on the vocal melody. There are scores of verses to "Hesitation Blues," many of them quite "R" rated. Compare this version with one by the Holy Modal Rounders (Fantasy FCD-24711-2), a young duo in the early 1960s, influenced by many of the same traditional musicians that Jerry and David listened to, that put their own stamp on the music.

Though Jerry doesn't take a lead guitar solo on "Hesitation Blues," I've transcribed his playing behind David's banjo solo.

Here's hoping you enjoy playing along with Jerry and David on a wonderful collection of great songs, brilliantly played by these two musical masters.

Dix Bruce

Shady Grove

D minor modal
Duet solo with mandolin

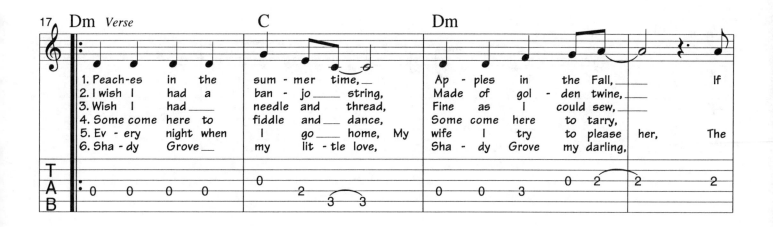

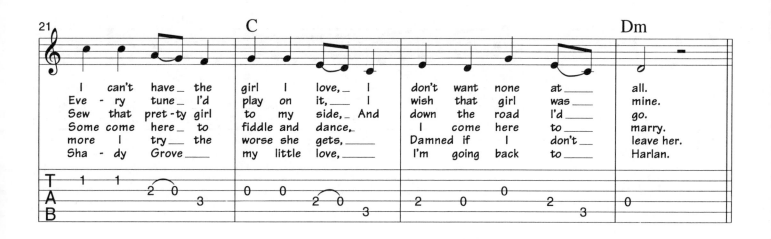

Chorus

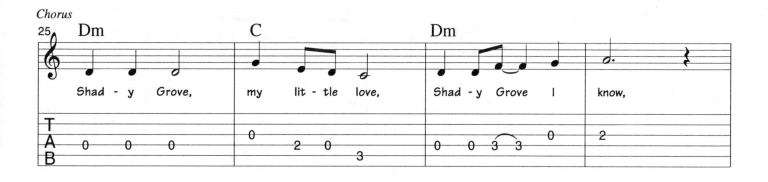

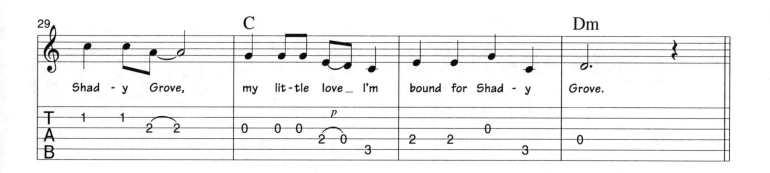

11

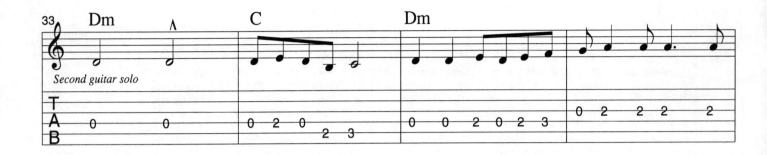

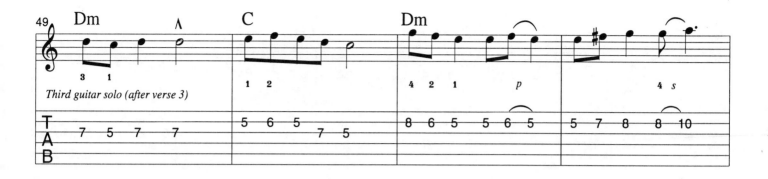

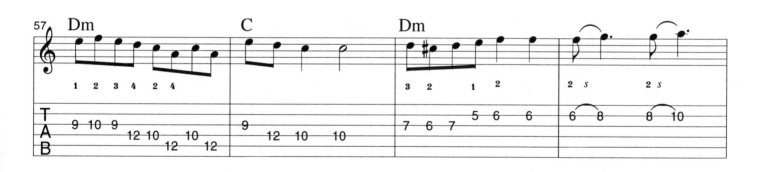

Guitar solo after verse 5

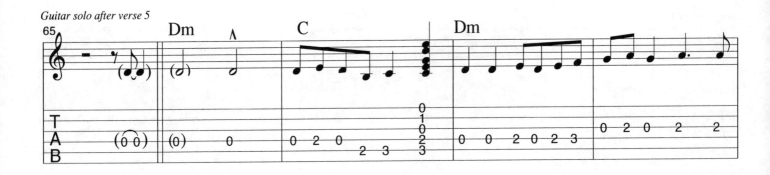

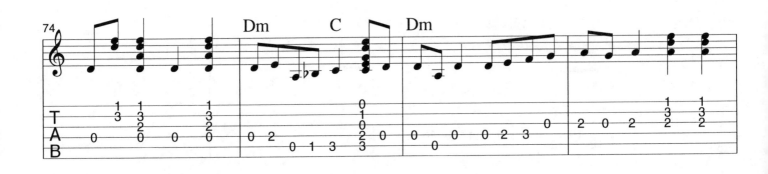

Dm vamp, chorus, last verse & cho
Last solo same as solo #1

*This page has been
left blank to avoid
awkward page turns*

Stealin'

Key of G

Intro solo

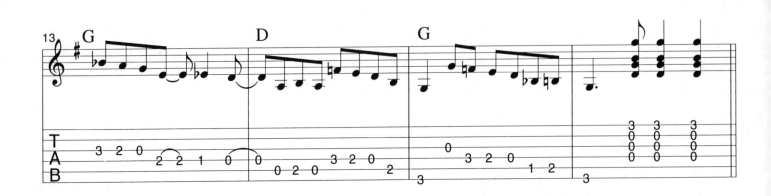

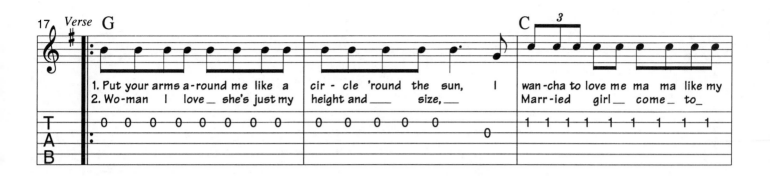

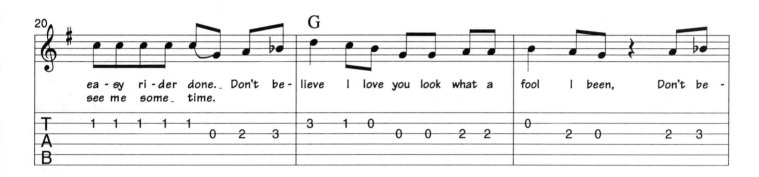

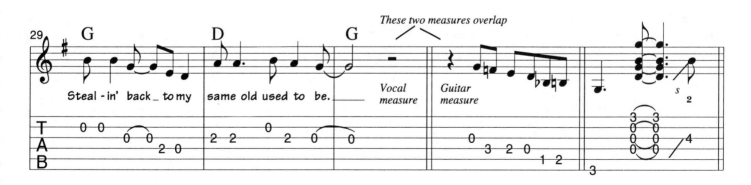

Guitar solo #1

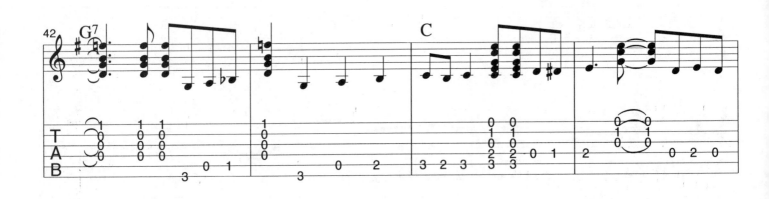

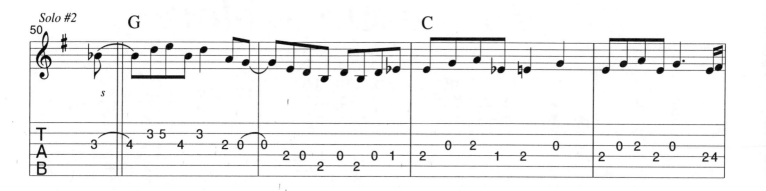

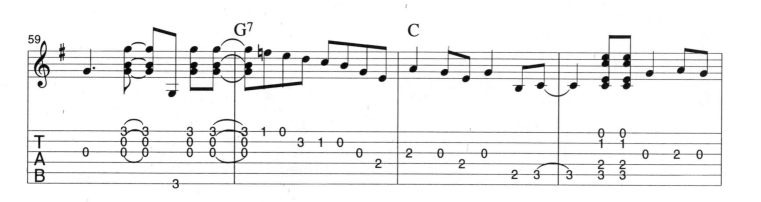

Repeat verse 1 then
chorus two times

Off to Sea Once More

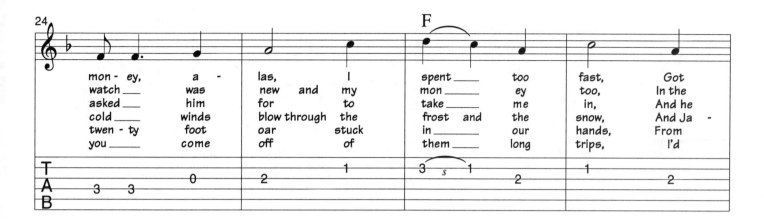

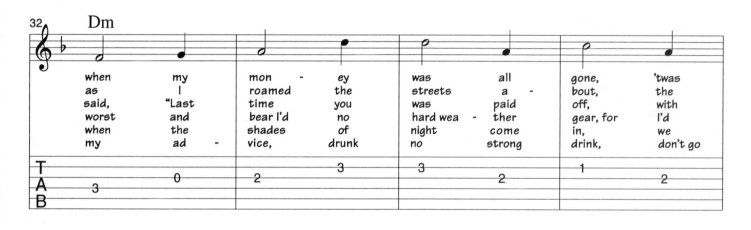

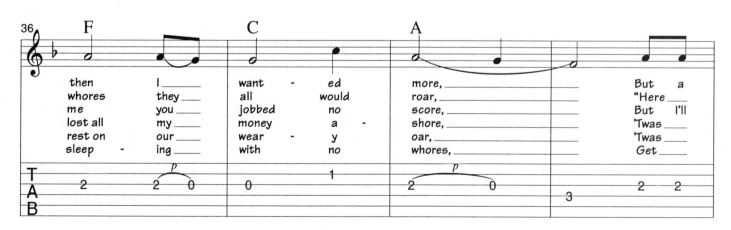

man must be	blind to	make up his	mind ____ to
comes ____ Jack	Rack, the	young sail - ing	lad, he must
take your ad -	vance and I'll	give ya's a	chance, ____ and I'll
then that I	wished that	I ____ was	dead, ____ so I'd
then ____ I	wished lads and	I ____ was	dead, ____ or
marr - i - ed	lads and have	all ____ night	in, ____ so you'll

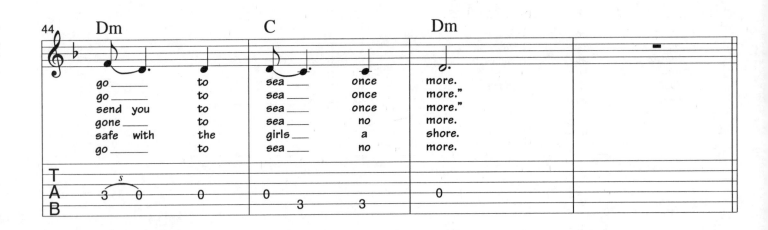

go ____ to	sea ____ once	more.	
go ____ to	sea ____ once	more."	
send you to	sea ____ once	more."	
gone ____ to	sea ____ no	more.	
safe with the	girls ____ a	shore.	
go ____ to	sea ____ no	more.	

Guitar & mandolin

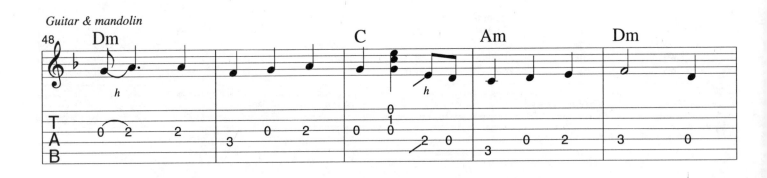

To 2nd verse

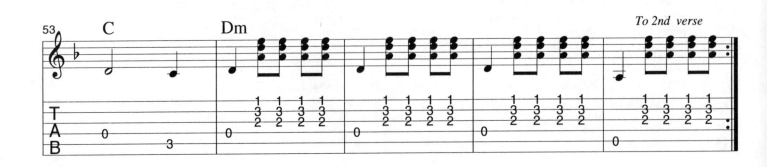

22

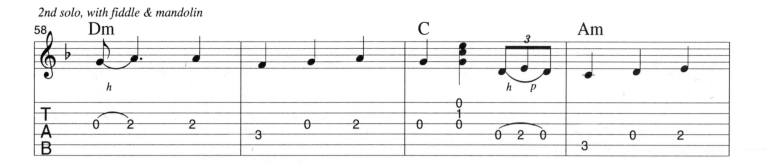

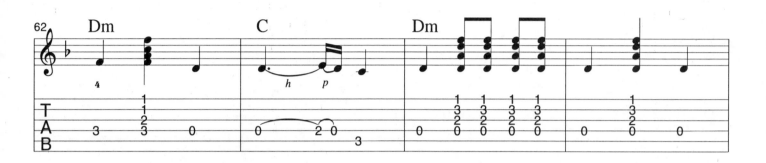

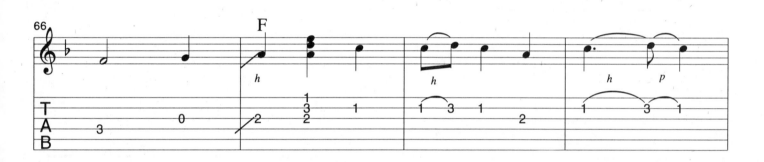

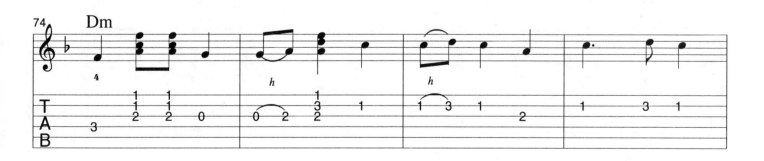

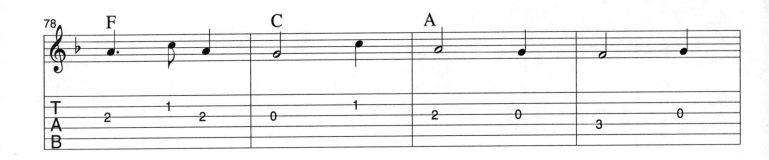

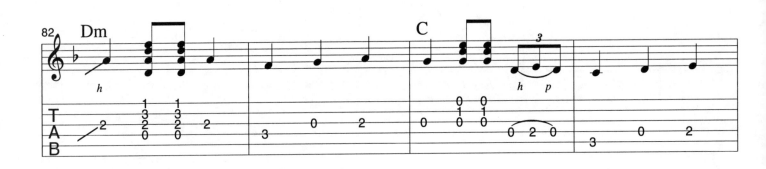

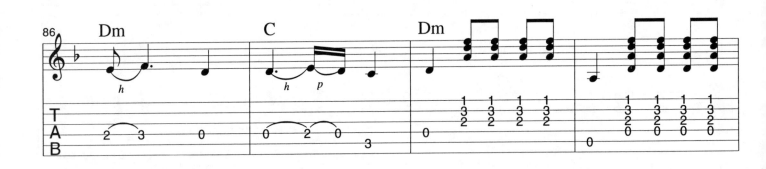

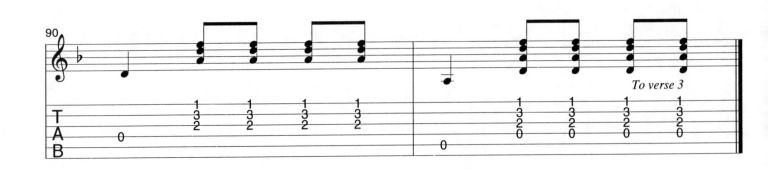

The Sweet Sunny South

Key of G
Intro based on banjo

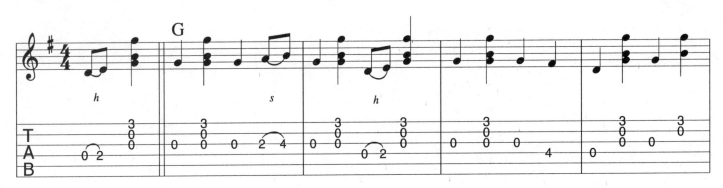

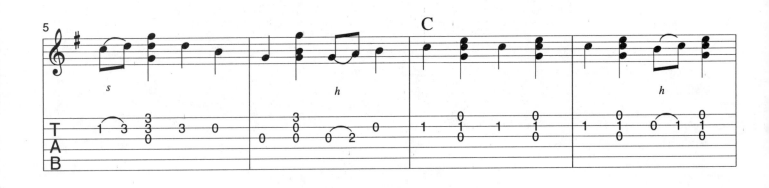

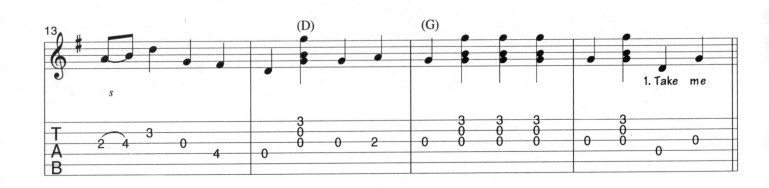

1. Take me

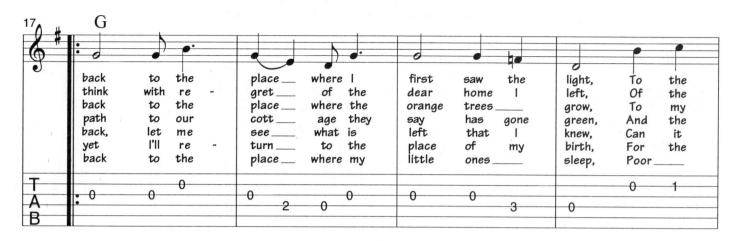

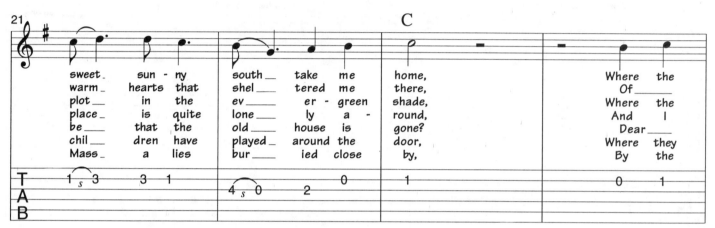

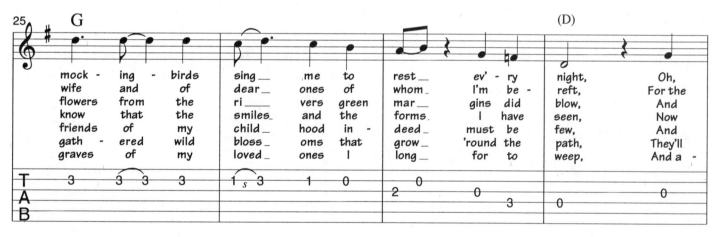

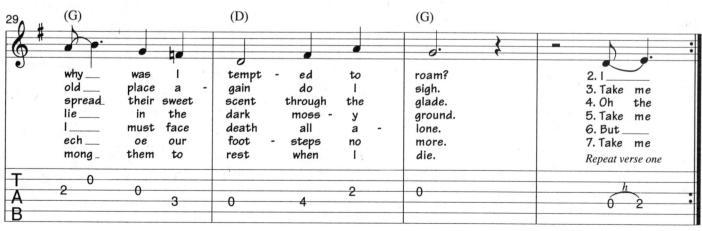

Louis Collins

John Hurt

Key of C
Guitar fingerpicked intro

Fair Ellender

Key of G
Guitar behind opening mandolin solo

6. She turned around all dressed in white, her sisters dressed in green,
And every town that they drove through, took her to be some queen.

7. They rode and they rode 'til they came to the hall, she pulled on the bell and it rang,
And no one so ready as Lord Thomas himself, to rise and welcome her in.

8. He taking her by her lily white hand, and leading her through the hall,
Saying "Fifty gay ladies are here today, but here is the flower of all."

9. The brown girl she was standing by, with knife ground keen and sharp,
Between the long ribs and the short, she pierced fair Ellender's heart.

10. Lord Thomas he was standing by, with knife ground keen and sharp,
Between the long ribs and the short, he pierced his own bride's heart.

11. By placing the handle against the wall, the point against his breast,
Saying "This is the end of three true lovers, God send us all to rest."

12. Father of father go dig my grave, go dig it wide and deep,
And place fair Ellender in my arms, the brown girl at my feet.

Turnaround after verse 1

Last guitar solo w/ mando

Jackaroo

Key of Em
Guitar intro

Verses:

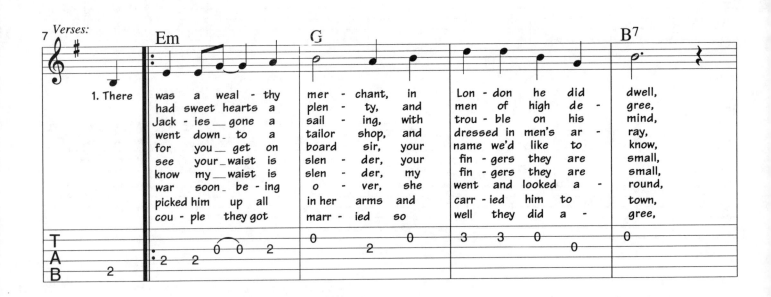

1. There was a weal - thy mer - chant, in Lon - don he did dwell,
   had sweet hearts a plen - ty, and men of high de - gree,
   Jack - ies __ gone a sail - ing, with trou - ble on his mind,
   went down __ to a tailor shop, and dressed in men's ar - ray,
   for you __ get on board sir, your name we'd like to know,
   see your __ waist is slen - der, your fin - gers they are small,
   know my __ waist is slen - der, my fin - gers they are small,
   war soon __ be - ing o - ver, she went and looked a - round,
   picked him up all in her arms and carr - ied him to town,
   cou - ple they got marr - ied so well they did a - gree,

He had a beau - ti - ful daugh __ ter the truth to you __ I'll
But none but Jack __ the sail __ or her true love __ there could
He left his na __ tive coun __ try and his dar - lin' __ girl be -
She climbed a - board __ a vess __ el to con - vey her __ self a -
She smiled in all __ her coun - ten - ence, "They call me __ 'Jack - a -
Your cheeks too red __ and ros __ y to face the __ can - non
My cheeks too red __ and ros __ y to face the __ can - non
A - mong the dead __ and wound __ ed her dar - lin __ boy she
She sent for a phy - sic __ ian who quick - ly heal his
This cou - ple they got marr __ ied so why not __ you and

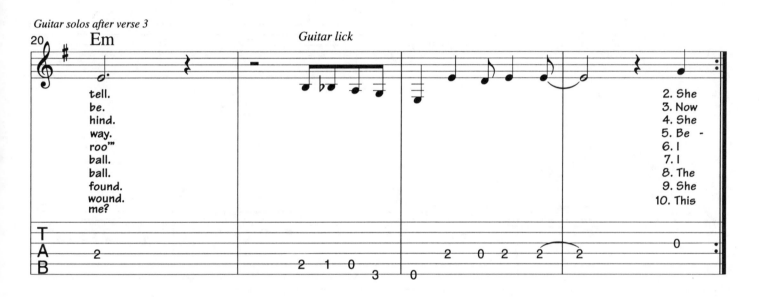

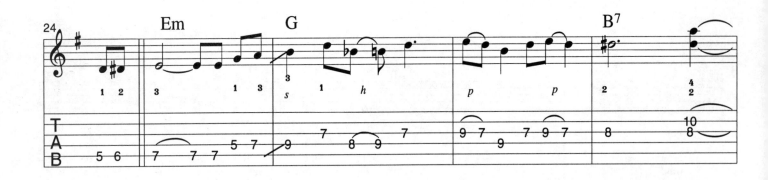

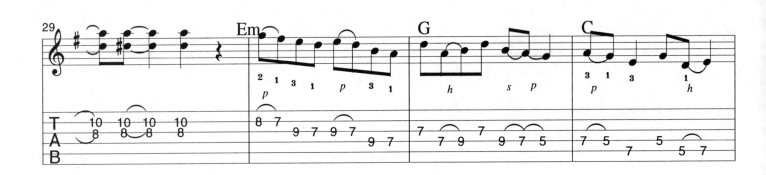

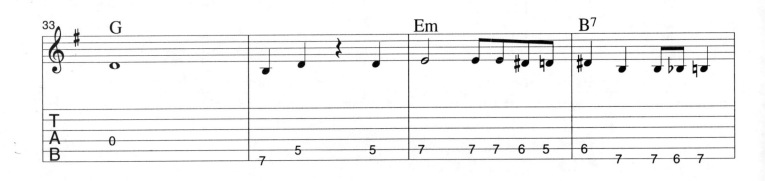

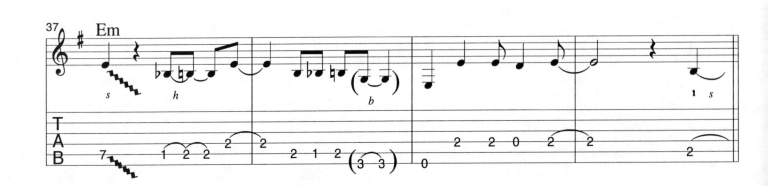

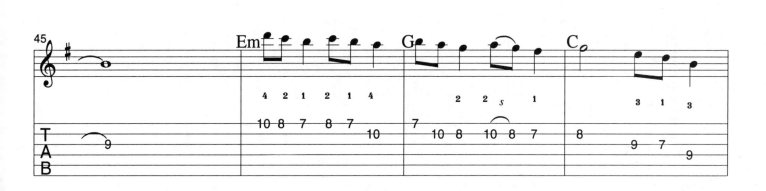

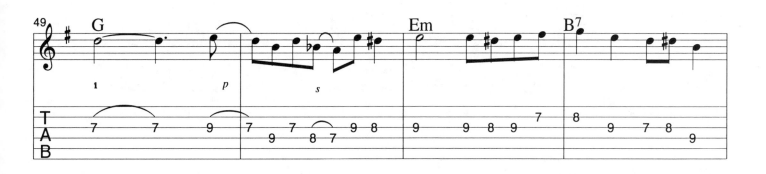

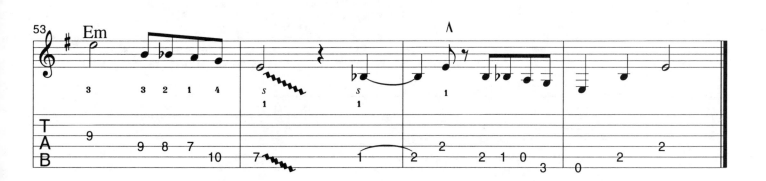

Casey Jones

Key of G
Fingerpicked guitar
Four measure intro

John Hurt

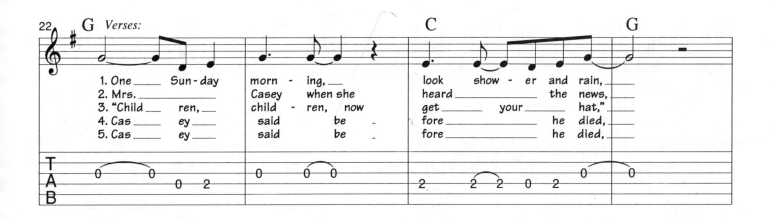

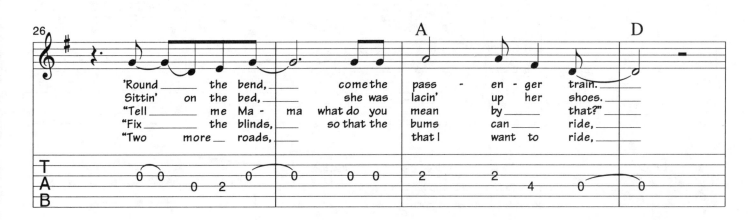

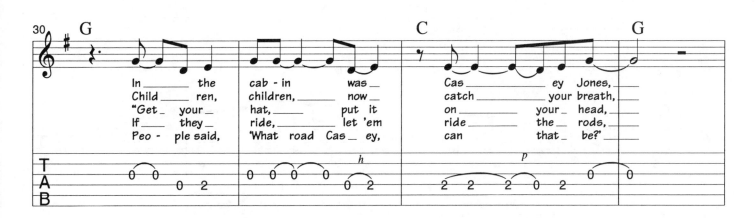

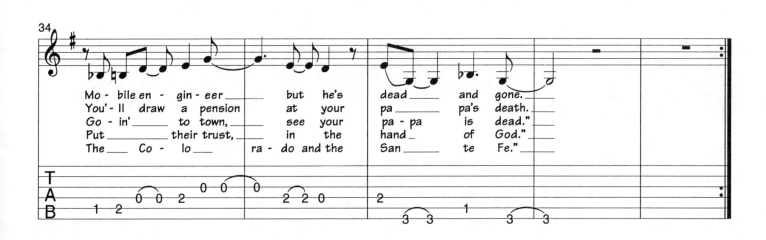

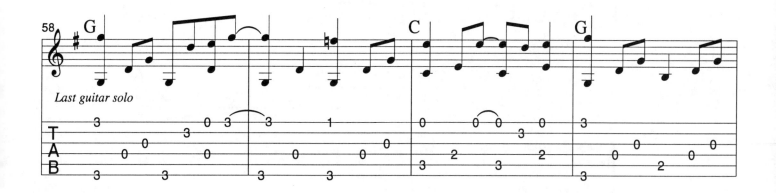

Last guitar solo

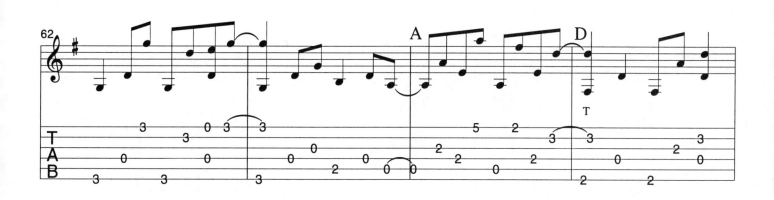

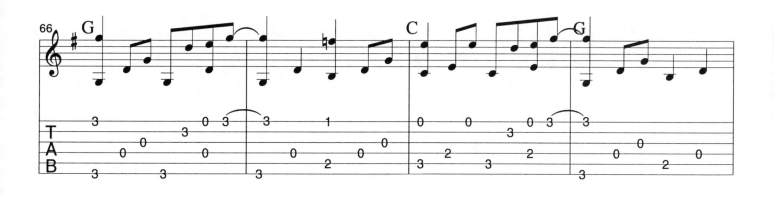

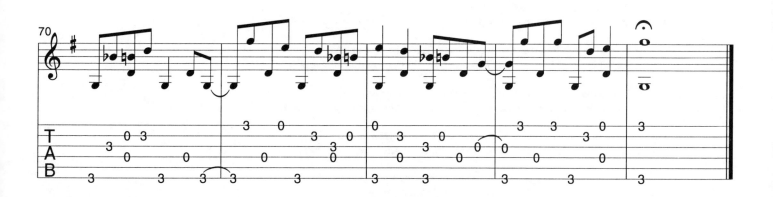

Dreadful Wind and Rain

Key of E
Verses:

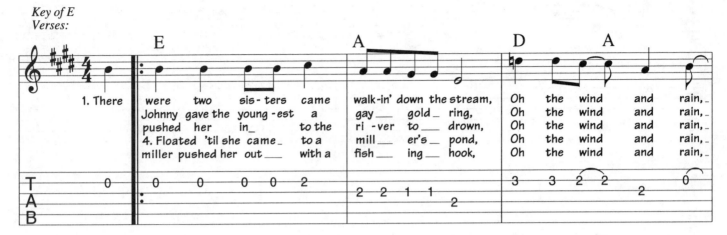

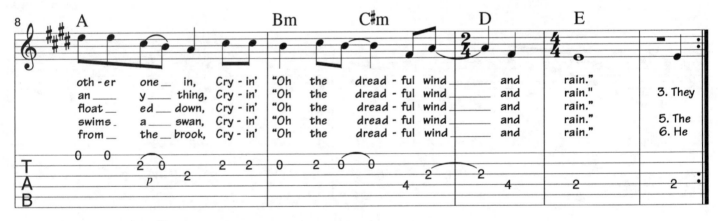

6. He left her on the banks to dry, cryin' "Oh the wind and rain,"
And a fiddlin' fool came passin' by, cryin' "Oh the dreadful wind and rain."

7. Out of the woods came a fiddler fair, oh the wind and rain,
Took thirty strands of her long yellow hair, cryin' "Oh the dreadful wind and rain."

8. And he made a fiddle bow of her long yellow hair, oh the wind and rain,
He made a fiddle bow of her long yellow hair, cryin' "Oh the dreadful wind and rain."

9. He made fiddle pegs of her long finger bones, oh the wind and rain,
He made fiddle pegs of her long finger bones, cryin' "Oh the dreadful wind and rain."

10. And he made a little fiddle of her breast bone, oh the wind and rain,
The sound could melt a heart of stone, cryin' "Oh the dreadful wind and rain."

11. And the only tune that fiddle would play was, "Oh the Wind and Rain,"
The only tune that fiddle would play was, "Oh the Dreadful Wind and Rain."

Solos after verse 3

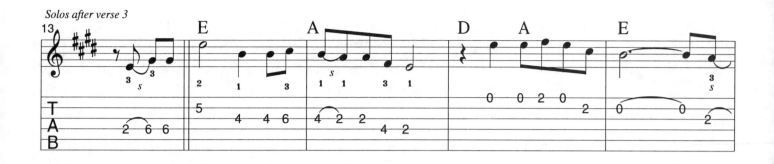

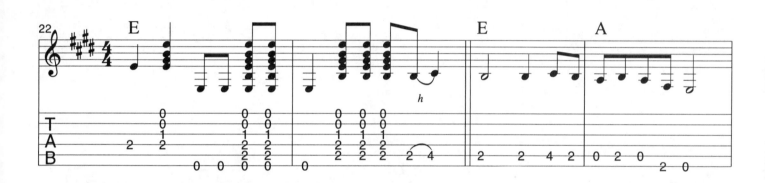

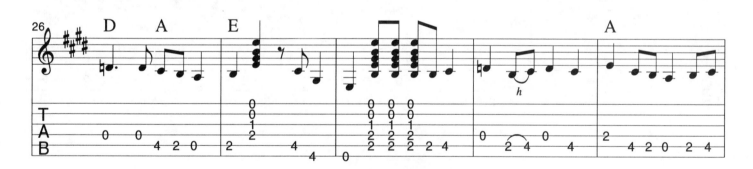

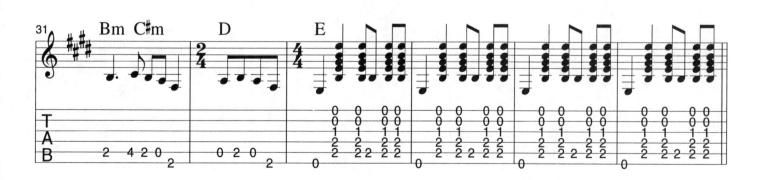

43

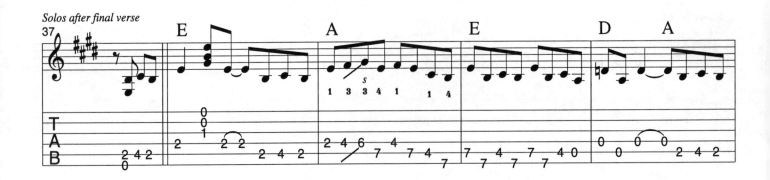

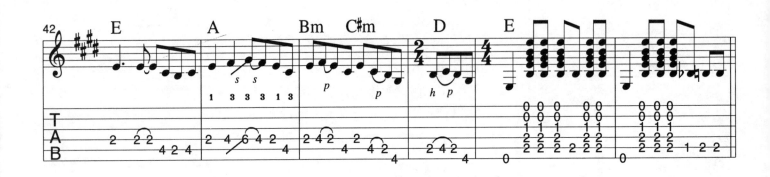

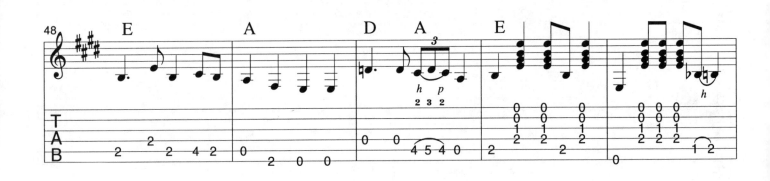

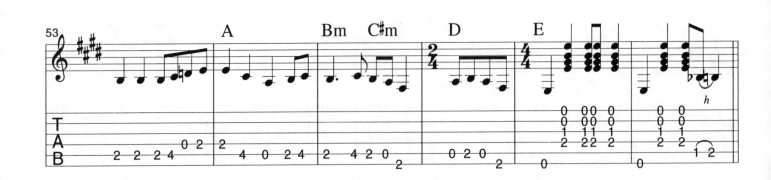

44

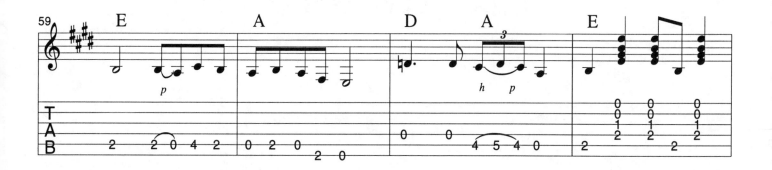

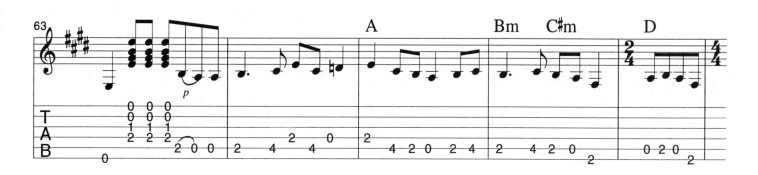

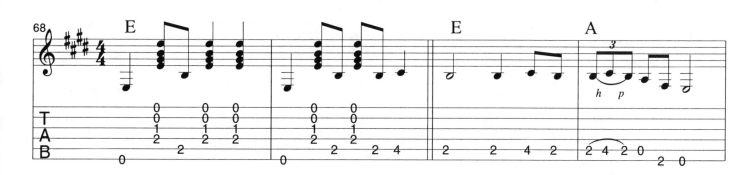

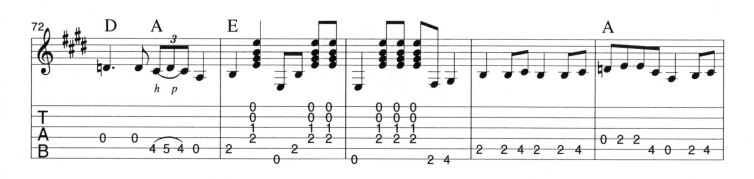

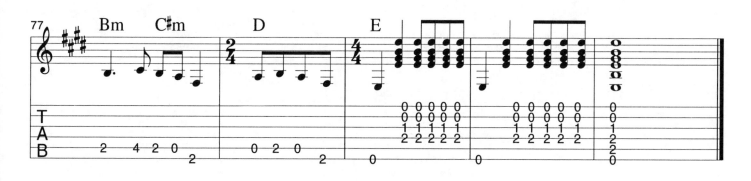

I Truly Understand

Key of G
Guitar solo based on Garcia & Grisman

Words and music
by George Roark

46

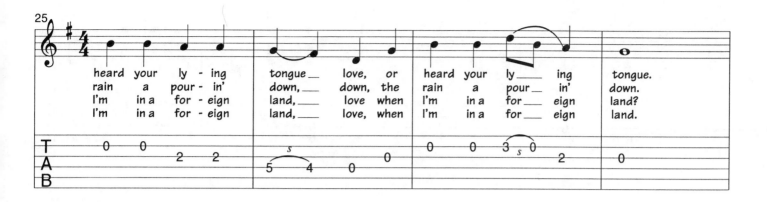

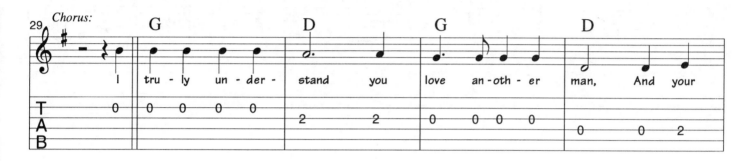

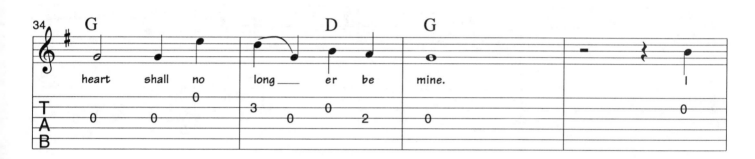

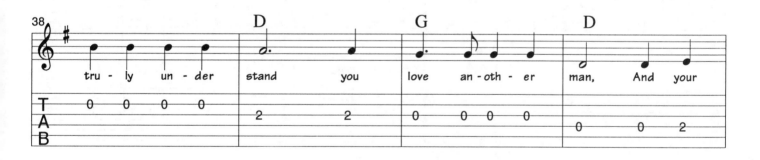

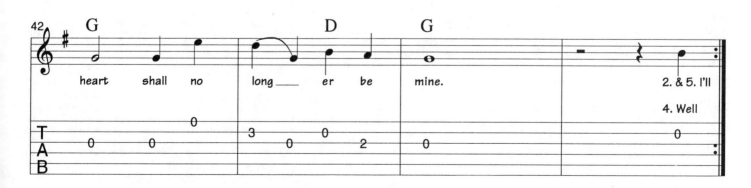

The Handsome Cabin Boy

Key of D

49

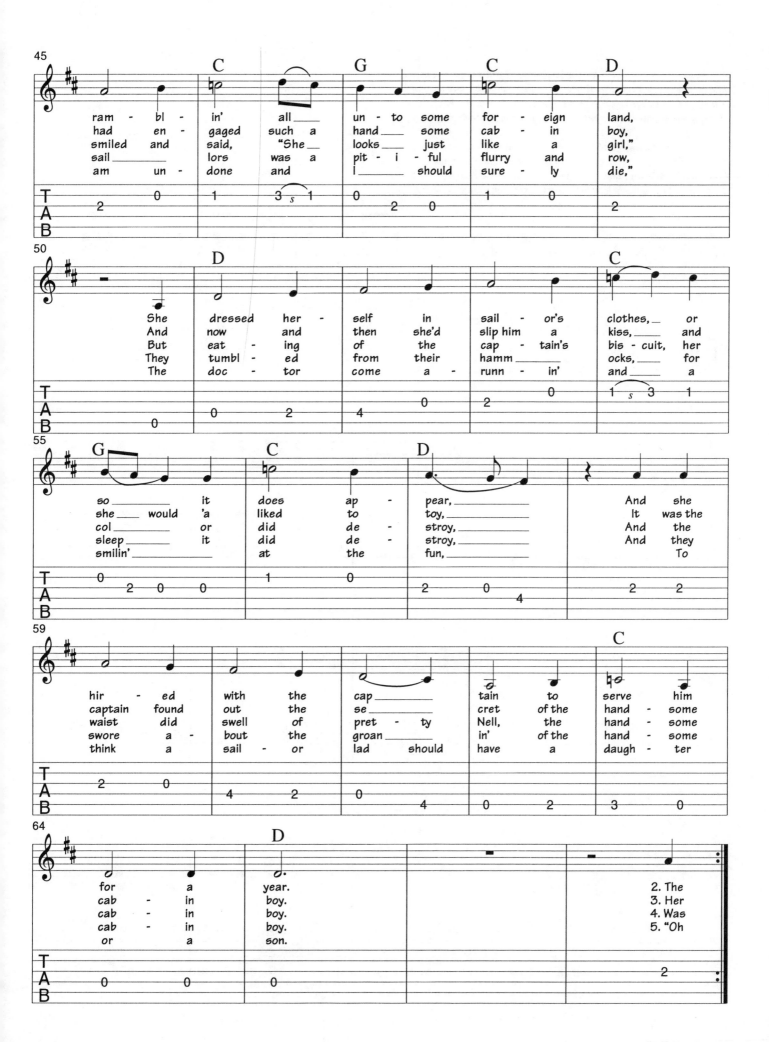

6. The sailors, when they saw the joke, they all did stand and stare,
The child belonged to none of them, they solemnly did swear,
The captain's wife, she says to him, "My dear, I wish you joy,
For it's either you or me's betrayed the handsome cabin boy."

7. So each man took his tote of rum, and he drunk success to trade,
And likewise to the cabin boy, who was neither man nor maid,
"Here's hoping wars don't rise again, our sailors to destroy,
And here's hoping for a jolly lot more like the handsome cabin boy."

Guitar solo after verse 2

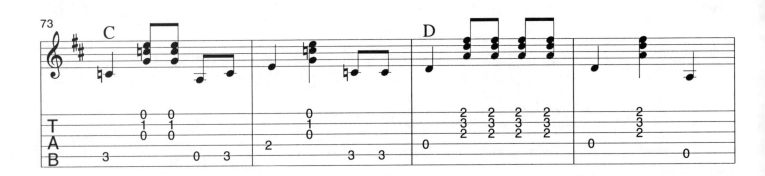

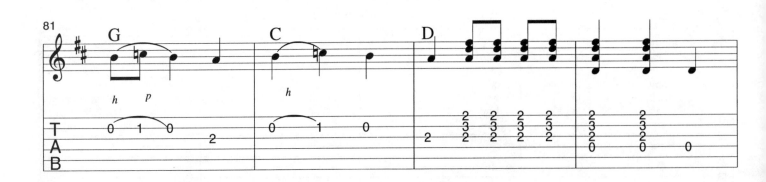

54

Ending

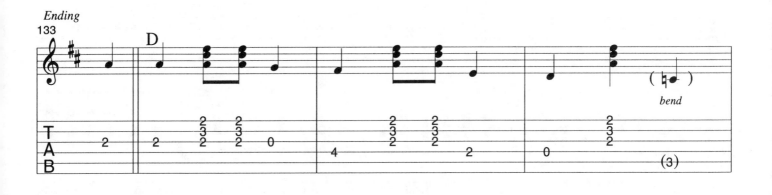

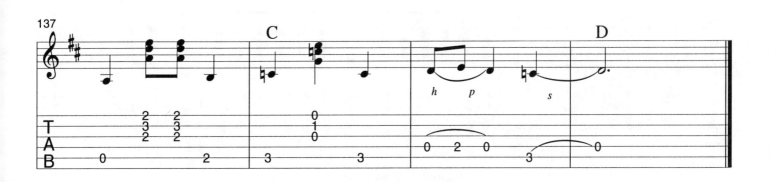

Whiskey in the Jar

Key of C
Guitar backup behind mandolin

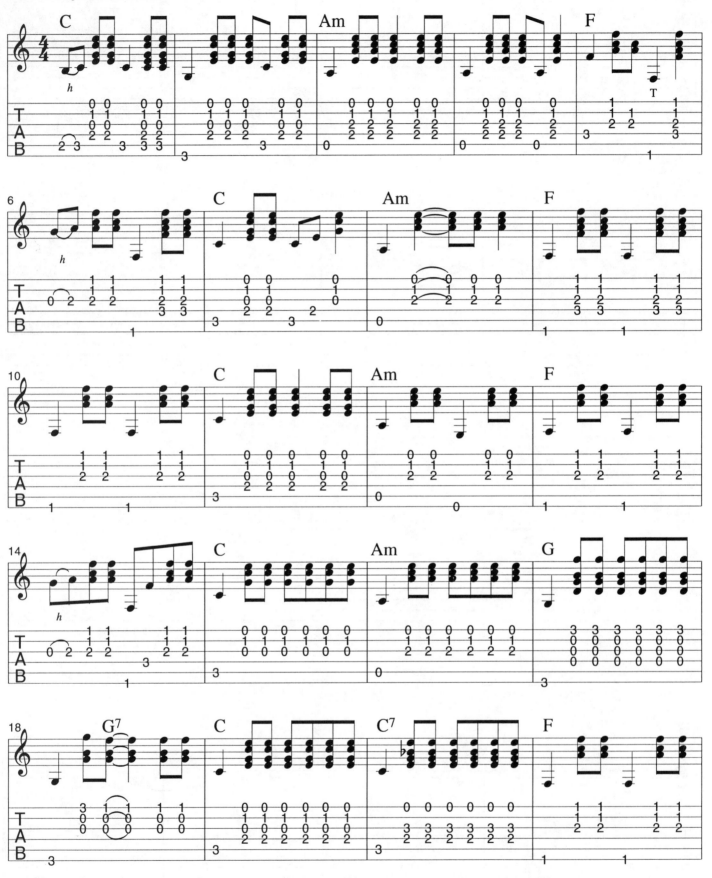

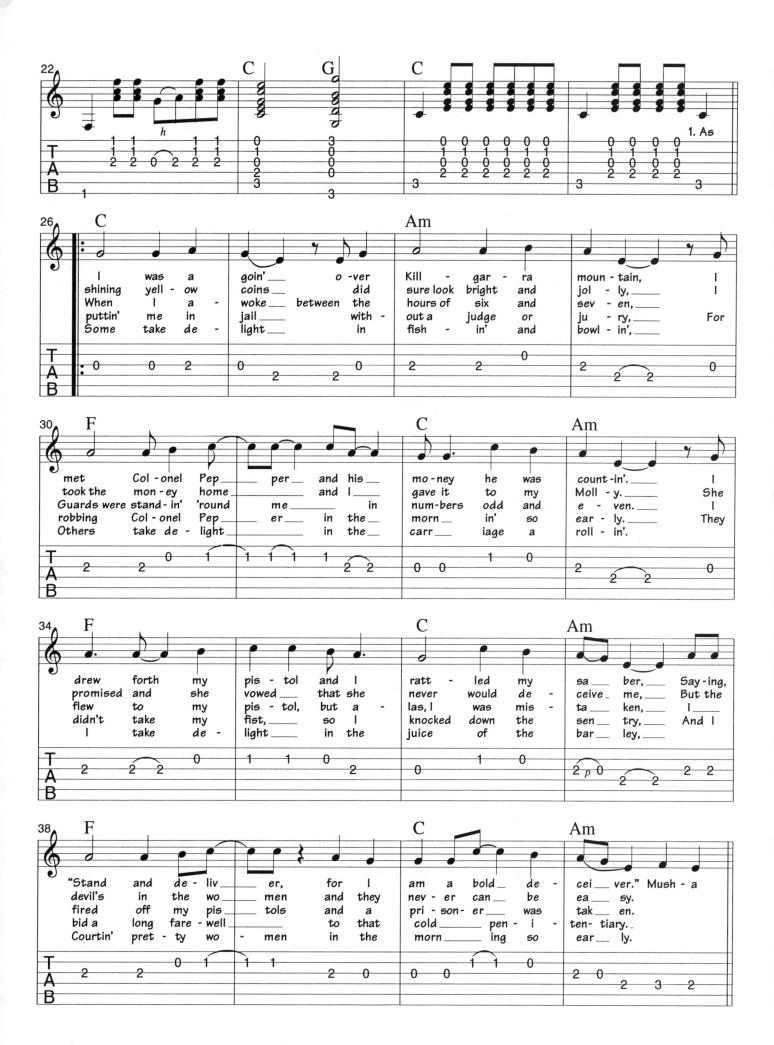

ring-um dur - am da, Whack! fol de die - di - o, ___

Whack! fol de die - di - o, ___ There's whis-key in the jar.

2. The

4. They

Guitar solo after Verse 2

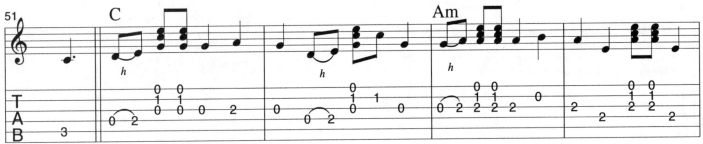

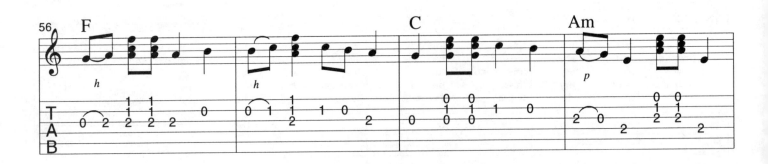

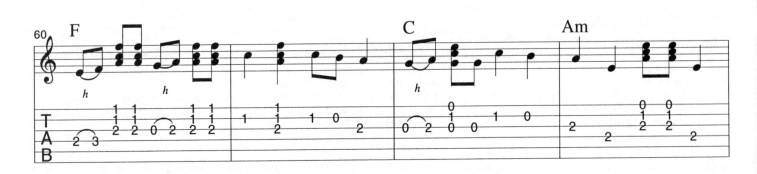

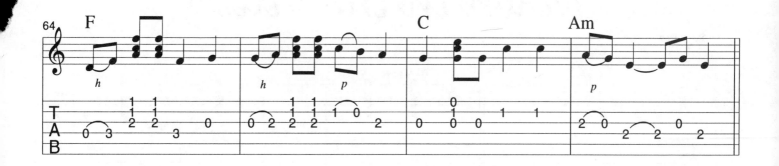

Guitar behind mandolin solo

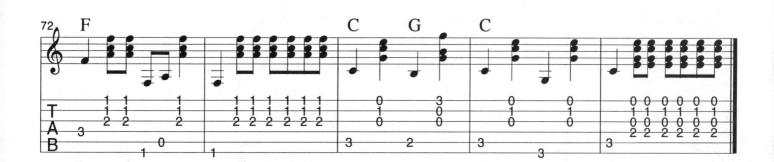

Down in the Valley

Key of G
Guitar intro

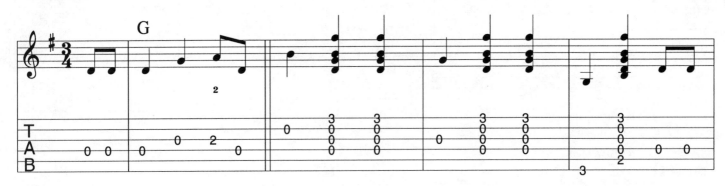

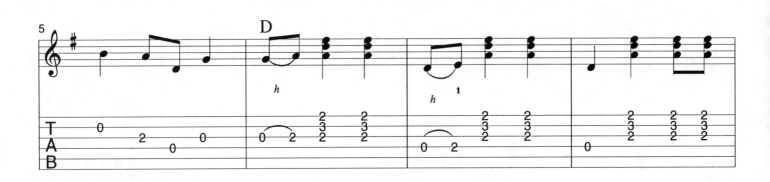

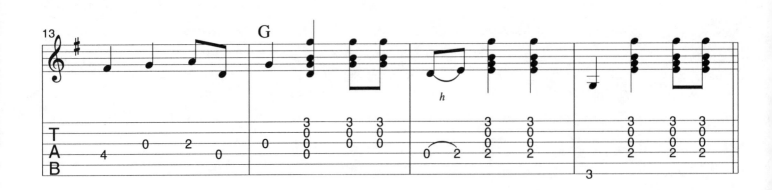

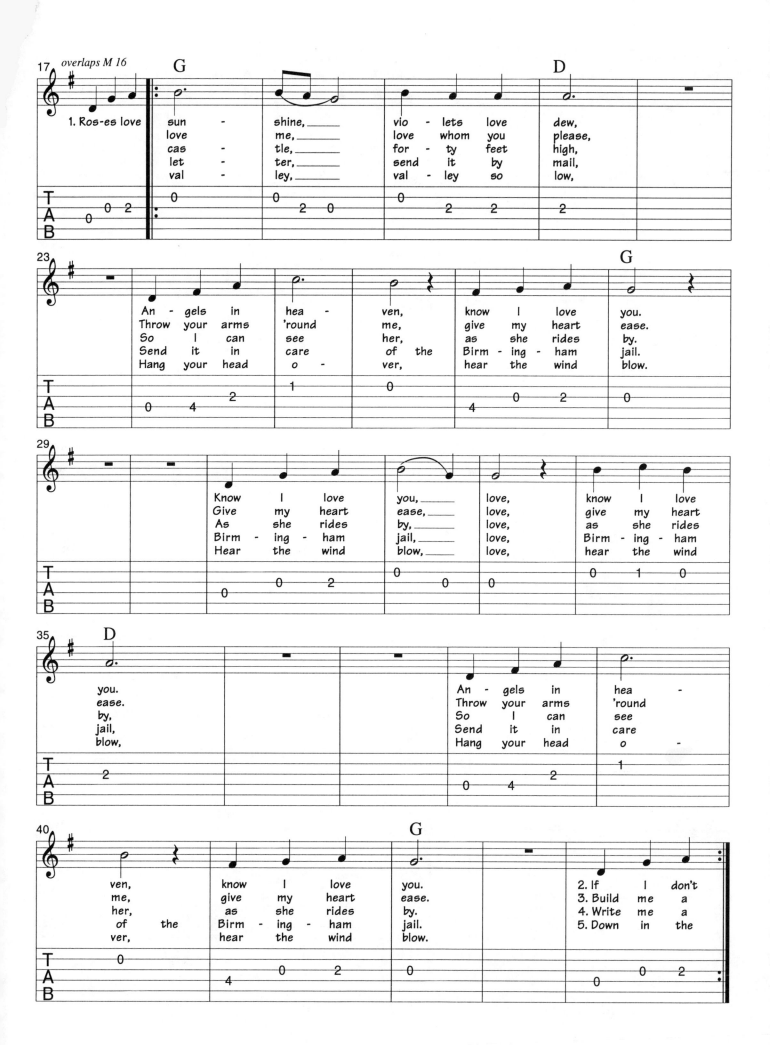

Hesitation Blues

Key of D
Fades in

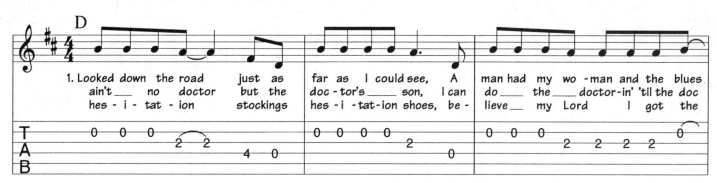

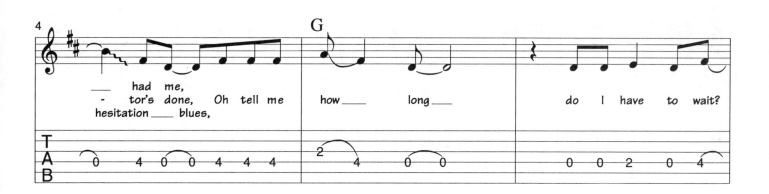

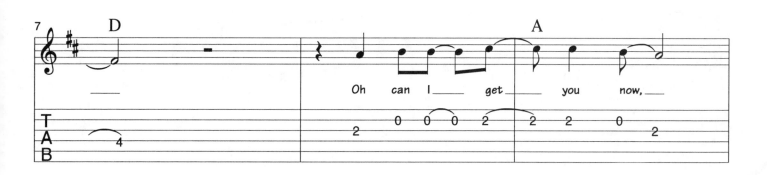

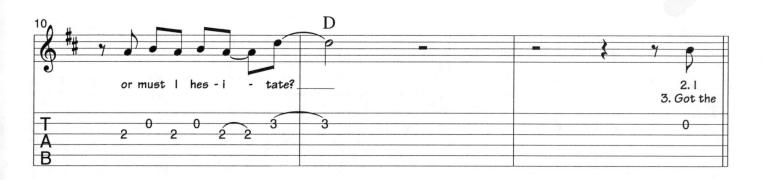

Backup behind Grisman

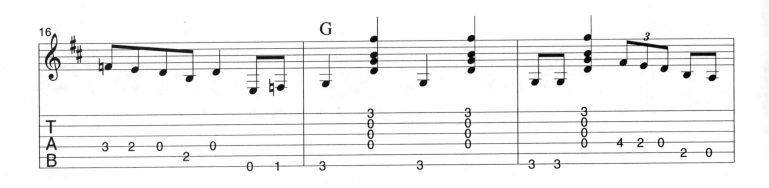

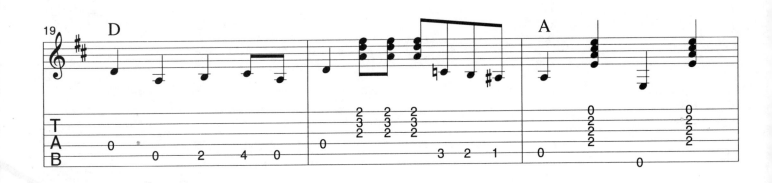

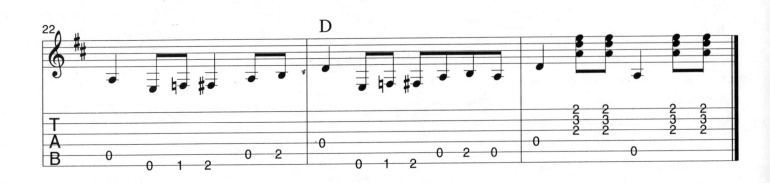